"Tower, we're ready."
"Okay, let's roll them off!"

Waddy climbed into the car through the window. Junior handed him the steering wheel, and Waddy clipped it into place on the steering column.

Waddy's crew chief, Cope, fastened yellow plastic mesh over the open window.

Amazing, thought Kin as he watched. *No door, no steering wheel, not even a window to roll up and down. Up close, stock car racing sure is odd!*

Kin had almost forgotten his hurt and disappointment in the excitement of preparing for the race.

The sky was bright blue, and the stands were filled with fans, all buzzing with anticipation. All that was missing was the race itself.

At that very moment, a voice came over the loudspeaker:

"Gentlemen, start your engines!"

Collect all the
NASCAR Pole Position Adventures:

#1 ROLLING THUNDER
#2 IN THE GROOVE
#3 RACE READY ·
#4 SPEED DEMON ·
#5 HAMMER DOWN ·

•coming soon

IN THE GROOVE

POLE POSITION ADVENTURES NO. 2

T.B. Calhoun

HarperEntertainment
An Imprint of HarperCollins*Publishers*

▥ HarperEntertainment

An Imprint of HarperCollins*Publishers*
10 East 53rd Street, New York, N.Y. 10022-5299

This is a work of fiction. The characters, incidents, and dialogues
are products of the author's imagination, or if real, are used ficti-
tiously. Any resemblance to actual events or persons, living or
dead, is entirely coincidental.

First Printing: October 1998

Cover illustration by John Youssi © 1998
Designed by Jeannette Jacobs

Printed in the United States of America.

ISBN 0-06-105937-4

HarperCollins®, ▥ ®, and HarperEntertainment are trademarks
of HarperCollins *Publishers* Inc.

Terry Labonte and the number 5 used with permission by
Hendrick Motorsports.

98 99 00 01 02 10 9 8 7 6 5 4 3 2 1

CONTENTS

NO BABY-SITTER NEEDED

Race day!

Kin Travis sat up straight in his narrow bed. His head almost bumped the low ceiling.

He was excited about something—but what?

Then he remembered. Today was race day.

The Pine Gap 300 was about to run—and he was going to be part of it!

He looked out the narrow window of the recreational vehicle where he had slept. Kin's grandfather, Hotshoe Hunter, was a retired NASCAR driver, and his big, boxy RV sat in the center of the infield parking lot at Pine Gap Raceway.

The stands that had been almost empty yesterday, for qualifying, were now already filling up with eager racing fans.

The race cars were still locked in the NASCAR

garage area, but the pits were already filling up with crew members. They were busy stacking tires, filling gasoline cans, preparing for the grueling but thrilling ordeal of a three-hundred-mile stock car race.

And today Kin Travis was going to be part of it all!

Laura Travis was having a dream. In the dream she was standing on the stage at Beacon Opera Hall in Boston. It had always been her ambition to sing opera—but she was wearing a strange outfit: boots and a cowgirl skirt!

The crowd was cheering wildly, and there in the front row were her mother and father—still alive, after all!

Laura's eyes filled with tears as she leaned forward and caught the bouquet her parents threw toward her.

Then she woke up.

She looked around the narrow, cramped little room at the back of her grandfather's RV.

It had all been a dream.

Her parents were dead, killed in a plane crash. She

was an orphan, along with her older brother, Kin, and her younger brother, Laptop.

They were at a stock car race track in the hills of East Tennessee. And the growing murmur of the crowd outside reminded her that it was race day!

Beep.

"Ouch!"

Larry "Laptop" Travis sat up and bumped his head.

He was in the tiny nook over the driver's seat of his grandfather's RV. It was barely big enough for him, and he was small for his age—eight.

Beep.

There it was again.

Laptop put his hand under his pillow and found his portable computer. It was an Apricot 07, an experimental model his father had completed right before leaving on his last trip.

There was something else under his pillow. A Civil War belt buckle—Laptop's proof (if anyone would listen) that ghosts were real.

Sort of, anyway.

Beep.

"Okay, okay!" Laptop left the buckle where it was, and pulled out the computer. He had programmed his Apricot 07 to turn itself on every morning, dial by cellular remote into his service, and check his e-mail messages. *Beep* meant he had messages waiting.

He opened the computer and scrolled through his e-mail.

Laptop had hundreds of e-mail friends around the world, from Russia to Africa to Korea to the South Pole (McMurdo.com).

Today he had ten messages, about average.

Most of them were just, "Hey, how are you?" "What's happening, dude?" and so forth.

But there was another mysterious message, just like the one he had gotten yesterday.

It was from GW at spirit.com.

It read: "WATCH THE SKIES."

"Good morning," said Kin, from his narrow bed on the couch.

"Good morning," said Laura, from her tiny bed at the rear of the RV.

"Good morning," said Laptop from his bed in the nook over the driver's seat.

"Good morning, kids," said Hotshoe Hunter, from his "bed" in the reclining driver's seat. Hotshoe was a man of about sixty with gray hair that needed cutting and a gray beard that needed trimming.

He wore a red and black hat pulled down over his eyes. The front of the hat advertised Merlin Mixmaster—Hotshoe's custom camshaft service.

He groaned and stretched.

Hotshoe Hunter had been a race driver in his youth. He had driven everything from late models to funny cars to street stocks, on dirt tracks and drag strips all over the Southeast. Now he followed the NASCAR stock car circuit in his RV, selling his custom-ground camshafts to the independents and the smaller racing teams.

"Well, kids," he said, sitting up. "Why don't one of you put up some coffee. Another pour the cereal. Another get out the milk and the bowls. Teamwork is everything. Let's have breakfast. It's race day!"

While the Travis kids and their grandfather

enjoyed breakfast, the Pine Gap Raceway was filling up.

Fans on foot were streaming into the grandstands, carrying coolers filled with soda and extra sandwiches, sunblock and ponchos against the heat and rain, scanners to eavesdrop on drivers and crews, binoculars, and signs supporting their favorite drivers—or attacking their archenemies.

Cars, vans, and trucks were streaming onto the infield, where they would park for the day.

"Today we have a three-hundred-miler," said Hotshoe between bites of corn flakes and gulps of steaming black coffee. "Pine Gap is a midsized track, only a mile and a quarter, so that's about three hundred laps."

"Two hundred and eighty," said Laptop, consulting his computer.

"The race won't take long, then," said Kin. "The qualifiers were running at over a hundred and sixty. Waddy Peytona won the pole position with 163.34."

Kin had made friends with Waddy Peytona's son, Junior. He had been invited to help the Peytona team during the race.

Laptop hit a few keys on his computer. "Three hundred divided by 163 . . . That means the race will last less than two hours—1.8366 hours to be exact," he reported.

Hotshoe laughed. "It's not that simple," he said. "The time trials are always faster than the race itself. For the race, you have to factor in cautions and pit stops."

"What are cautions?" Laura asked. "Like caution lights?"

"Sort of," said Hotshoe. "A caution is a yellow flag. If there's a wreck or a problem on the track, maybe oil or debris or a broken-down car, the NASCAR officials wave a yellow flag. All the cars have to slow down and hold their positions until the green flag is waved."

"And pit stops are for gas and tires," said Kin. "Every car will have to make at least three."

"The race will probably last closer to three hours," said Hotshoe. "It's supposed to start at noon." He looked at his watch. "It's almost nine. I have to go by the garage and get some work done. I want you kids to stay out of the way and look after one another."

"I'm going to be helping Waddy Peytona's team," said Kin. "I won't be able to look after Laptop."

"I don't need anybody to look after me!" Laptop protested loudly.

"I'm going to be helping Infield Annie," said Laura. Infield Annie had a food concession stand. "I won't be able to look after Laptop."

"I don't need anybody to look after me!" Laptop protested again, even more loudly.

"You should watch the race, too," Hotshoe said to Laura. "It's your first race. You might even like it."

"Phooey," said Laura. "Cars going around in a circle? What do I care!"

"You might be surprised," said Hotshoe with a grin. He turned to the youngest of his three grand-children. "So what's the story, Laptop? Who's going to look after you?"

"I told you, I don't need a baby-sitter," said Laptop. "I'm eight years old. I'm perfectly capable of looking after myself."

"Well, okay," said his grandfather, getting up from the tiny table and readjusting the MERLIN hat he never took off, even to sleep. "Just stay out of trouble."

"Worf!" said Scuffs, the little yellow dog who had adopted the Travis kids for his own.

"You too, Scuffs," said Hotshoe. He started out the door, then stopped with his hand on the knob.

"One more thing. A couple of obnoxious bill collectors have been calling me. So if the phone rings, *don't* answer it."

URGENT MESSAGE

No sooner had Hotshoe shut the door behind him than the phone rang.

Kin looked at Laura.

Laura looked at Laptop.

Laptop looked at Scuffs.

Scuffs looked back at Kin—or McKinley, the oldest in the family. It was Kin who had first adopted the little yellow dog and given him his name.

"Worf!" said Scuffs.

"Don't you dare," said Kin, wagging his finger at the dog. "We're not supposed to answer it."

The phone rang four times, then the answering machine picked up.

"You have reached the international corporate headquarters of Merlin MixMaster Camshaft

Wizardry," said Hotshoe's recorded voice. "Please leave a message after the honk."

A horn honked.

Laura winced.

Laptop laughed.

"Corn-ee!" said Kin.

"Mr. Hunter?" said a familiar—at least to the kids—voice. "This is Adrian Emerson in Boston, the children's aunt and legal guardian. There has been an unforeseen change in plans, and I need to speak to you about the children's summer plans, urgently. Please call me ASAP."

She clicked off.

"What's ASAP?" asked Laptop.

"Fast!" said Kin.

"As Soon As Possible," said Laura. "We'd better go and find Grandpa Hotshoe!"

From the infield, Kin, Laura, and Laptop could see that the race track was surrounded by green Tennessee hills, dotted with little barns and fields of tobacco, hay, and corn.

Behind the green hills loomed the bulk of

Rockcastle Mountain, named for the steep limestone cliffs that crowned the ridge.

The hills were alive with the sound of cars. Racing fans were streaming into the Pine Gap Raceway. They came across the valley from the south, through the woods from the east, and down the mountains to the south and west.

They came from cities and small towns, from as close as Kentucky and Virginia, and from as far away as Illinois, South Carolina, and Missouri.

All the roads snaking down across the green Tennessee hills were jammed and clotted with cars.

Classic cars from the fifties, like Hotshoe's precious '55 Chevy, were mixed with pickup trucks, custom hot rods, sedate Japanese sedans, sleek German touring cars, and a variety of the latest Detroit iron.

"I got another weird e-mail from spirit.com!" said Laptop as he followed his brother and sister hurrying across the infield toward the big garage, where they hoped to find their grandfather. "This one said 'Watch the skies.' Yesterday it was 'Find a friend'—and I did!"

"You mean your imaginary friend?" said Kin. "That's ridiculous!"

"Yes, him!" Laptop said defiantly. Laptop had made friends with a bona fide Civil War ghost—though nobody would believe him. "And there's nothing ridiculous about him."

"Is he a Confederate ghost or a Union ghost?" Laura asked.

"He can't remember," said Laptop. "He remembers fighting in a battle, but he can't remember which side he was on."

"Ridiculous," Kin said again.

"You two quit bickering," said Laura. "Maybe the e-mail means something. Maybe you should tell Hotshoe."

"It's too weird," said Laptop. "Grown-ups don't like weird. They always overreact."

"Maybe it's just stupid kids' stuff," said Kin, making it clear that that's exactly what he thought it was.

"Don't walk so fast!" said Laptop, struggling to keep up.

As always, he carried his portable computer clutched under one arm.

There was a huge crowd outside the gates of the

garage area. It was mostly mechanics and crew members anxious to get in and work on their cars. The garage was closed and locked by NASCAR officials at night, after the cars were inspected for the race. It opened at six A. M. sharp. That gave the drivers and crews only a few hours to fine-tune their cars for the race.

NASCAR officials were just unlocking the gate when the kids approached. The eager mechanics and crew members streamed in, almost knocking the kids down.

"Whoah!" said Laura, pulling Laptop out of the way.

"I don't need a baby-sitter!" he protested.

"We've got passes, we can go in," said Kin. "Come on!"

The big garage was divided into work areas. Each area held a car hauler—some of them shiny and brand new; others, well, not so new but still shiny. Each area also held a race car.

There were Fords, Pontiacs, Chevrolets—all brightly painted, polished and gleaming.

Even as the kids entered, the first of the engines were coughing and sputtering as the mechanics started them up for fine-tuning.

BBRRROOOOM!

BBRRROOOOM!

BBRRROOOOM!

The racket in the garage area was incredible. It put a smile on Kin's face, and a frown on Laura's.

"There he is!" Laptop yelled.

Hotshoe Hunter was in the far corner of the garage, bending over a black and red Pontiac. The hood was up and the engine was racing as Hotshoe studied a vacuum gauge.

"You have a phone call!" Laura yelled.

Hotshoe smiled and nodded distractedly.

"It's from Aunt Adrian!"

Hotshoe smiled and nodded and went back to studying the engine vacuum.

"She wants you to call her ASAP!"

Hotshoe smiled . . .

"Later!" shouted Kin, grabbing his sister's arm and pulling her over to a quieter corner. "Grandpa Hotshoe's working. We shouldn't disturb him before the race."

"I guess you're right," said Laura. "Let's get out of here! The noise is killing me!"

— — — — — — — — — — — — — — — —

"Really?" said Kin, looking surprised. "I think it's beautiful!"

Outside the garage area, cars were still streaming across the track into the infield. Most of them were pickups and campers, family cars and station wagons, with a few hot rods and sports cars mixed in.

Then there was a long line of shiny old cars. Instead of heading for the parking lot, they turned off under a banner that read:

CRUISIN' CLASSICS
GOLDEN OLDIES INFIELD CAR SHOW

"Neat!" said Laptop. "For antiques, that is."

"They're beautiful," said Laura. "I never particularly liked cars before, but these look like costume jewelry, with all that chrome and bright colors."

And indeed they did.

There was a salmon pink and charcoal 1956 Ford convertible; a blue and white 1954 Buick Century, said to be the first American production car capable of 100 mph speeds off the showroom floor; a red and black

1955 Lincoln, the legendary Mexican Road Race winner. There were 1950 Fords with lowered springs and frenched headlights; a whale-like 1951 Mercury with fender skirts and dual exhausts, like the one Dennis Hopper drove off a cliff in his *Rebel Without a Cause* "chicken" race with James Dean.

It even had fuzzy dice hanging from the rearview mirror!

All the classic cars were driven into a roped-off area of the infield, not far from the Winner's Circle.

The next-to-last car in line was a familiar-looking 1955 Chevrolet Belair two-door hardtop.

"That's Grandpa Hotshoe's Chevy!" shouted Laptop excitedly.

And Kin's new friend, Junior, was at the wheel!

"I promised your granddad I would drive his car in," said Junior, a little apologetically. "He's busy setting up his drivers for the race, and I'm not needed in the pits until the race starts."

"I could have driven the car in," said Kin resentfully. "It has automatic transmission."

"You don't have a license," said Junior. "I'm only six months older than you, but being sixteen makes all the difference."

"I guess it does," said Kin grimly. Sometimes it seemed that everybody in the world got to drive but him!

The last car in the line of classics pulled in.

"Wow!" said Junior.

Even Laura said, "Woooo!"

"What kind of car is that?" Kin asked.

It was a small, sleek two-door with a tiny back seat; almost a coupe. It had a square grille like a Mercedes, and huge swooping fins on the rear fenders. The fins were inlaid with what looked like gold foil.

"That's Wild Bill's Studebaker," said Junior. "He's a good friend of my dad and your grandpa."

"A what-a-baker?" asked Laptop.

"They don't make Studies anymore," said Junior. "Studebaker went out of business in about 1957. Wild Bill's car is a Golden Hawk. It was one of the first American attempts at a sports car. Sort of like the Thunderbird and the Corvette—except that it didn't catch on."

"It would have if Studebaker hadn't gone out of business," said the driver, getting out. He was a big, thick man smoking a big, thick cigar. "The Hawk was a great car, ahead of its time."

The smell of the cigar made Laura want to gag. She waved her hands in front of her nose. "Please!"

"Excuse me!" said the man. "I'm the owner of this little jewel. Bill Wilde's the name, but you can call me—"

"Wild Bill, we know," said Kin, shaking the big man's hand. "I'm Kin Travis, and this is Laura and Laptop."

"Oh, I know!" said Wild Bill. "You are Hotshoe's favorite grandchildren."

"We're his *only* grandchildren," said Laptop.

"Same thing," said Wild Bill.

"You know about us?" Kin asked, surprised.

"I've heard of nothing else!" said Wild Bill Wilde. "Hotshoe's been bragging on you-all for months. He's even talked me into offering you a ride in the pace car, when the race starts."

"Not you, Kin!" said Junior, grabbing Kin's arm. "You're going to help us in the pits, remember? You and I had better get going. It's our job to straighten up the pit area before we roll the car out. And the race starts at noon!"

"Worf!" said Scuffs.

-- -- -- -- -- -- -- -- -- -- -- -- -- -- --

"Oh, all right," said Junior, leaning down and scratching the little dog between the ears. "You can come, too. Just make sure you stay out of the way!"

CLOUD SPLITTERS

"Look!" said Laura.

She was standing with Wild Bill and Laptop by the Studebaker Golden Hawk. She pointed to the top of Rockcastle Mountain. Four jets streaked over the ridge top, flying in formation, as silent and as graceful as bats.

Streaming white smoke, they flew over the infield, then rocketed straight up, splitting in four directions like a flower blossoming.

Right behind them came their sound—a wave like thunder.

BBAAAARRRRROOOOOOM!

"Wow!" said Laptop.

"Ooooooh!" shouted the crowd in the grandstand, apparently agreeing.

It was the Air National Guard aerobatics team. All

four jets flew straight up until they were just dots, then disappeared in a puff of red, white, and blue smoke.

Out of the smoke, four shapes fell, streaming smoke and falling, falling . . .

"Aaaaah!" sighed the crowd.

Four parachutes opened. They were rectangles— one red, one white, one blue, and one silver.

The parachutists crisscrossed in and out, in and out, steering down in a corkscrew pattern toward the Pine Gap Raceway.

"They're going to land in the infield!" said Laura.

The fans in the grandstand were cheering wildly as the parachutists circled, getting closer and closer to the ground.

They were aiming for the Winner's Circle, just past the pits.

"How can they steer?" Laptop asked Wild Bill.

"They're called para-gliders," said Wild Bill Wilde. "They steer with the ropes. Pull to the left to go left, and pull to the right to go right. It's simple. Not that I've ever tried it—or ever would!"

The jets streaked again low over the field, just as

the parachutists hit the ground running. Then the jets blasted up over the top of Rockcastle Mountain and out of sight.

The air show was over.

Or was it?

"Look!" said Laura.

A blimp motored slowly over the grandstand, toward the infield.

The blimp was silver, and except for a scarlet lightning bolt painted on the side, it carried no markings or ads of any kind.

"Strange," said Wild Bill. "But it must be part of the air show."

"Must be," agreed Laura. She liked blimps better than jets. They weren't as noisy.

As the blimp cruised quietly over the Cruisin' Classics Golden Oldies area, a door opened in the gondola attached to the bottom of the blimp.

Two figures fell out.

"Ooohhhh!" went the crowd in the grandstand.

Two rectangular chutes opened. Two para-gliders came down, circling in and out like the first four had done.

The crowd in the grandstand applauded.

The two parachutists touched down in the infield, not far from the car show area.

One was a man and one was a woman. Both had short blond hair and wore gray spandex tights. The man was carrying a canvas bag.

The two parachutists gathered up their chutes and folded them. Then they took some clothing out of the bag—and something that looked suspiciously like a gun.

"Are you sure they're part of the air show?" Laptop asked.

"Of course," Laura said. "What else could they be?"

"Air show's over anyway!" said Wild Bill impatiently. "Why don't you kids come with me, and let's crank up the pace car and start the race."

"You mean it's up to us?" asked Laura.

"You bet!" said Wild Bill. "Well, us and NASCAR. When everybody is in place and the cars are warmed up, NASCAR gives the signal and we roll off the pit road."

"Awesome!" said Laptop. Clutching his computer, he followed Wild Bill and Laura toward the Cruisin' Classics car show area.

IN THE LAND OF OZ

"I can't believe we have to push this thing!" said Kin. He and Junior were helping to push Waddy Peytona's Ford out of the garage. "Doesn't it have an engine?"

"You bet it has an engine," said Waddy, who walked alongside, conserving his energy for the race. "It has about thirty thousand dollars' worth of engine. We don't use it for little stuff like getting from the garage to the pits."

"Running slow is hard on a racing engine," said Tach, the team's head mechanic.

"It's hard on the clutch, too," said Cope, the crew chief.

"Besides," said Waddy, "pushing together gives the crew a chance to get warmed up and get in the spirit of working together."

They all groaned. But kept pushing.

In spite of his complaints, which were only for show, Kin loved being part of the team. He was beaming with pleasure as they rolled the race car toward the pits, under the bright Tennessee sunshine.

Outside the garage area, Scuffs greeted him with a happy bark.

Kin was amazed at how light the car was and how easily it rolled. The sheet metal was so thin that it almost bent when he touched it.

The body of Waddy Peytona's Taurus was only for show. A lightweight body on an all-out racing frame, it was a stock Taurus in appearance only.

"Grab a piece of frame," said Junior. "The fenders dent too easily."

If they dent from just leaning on them, Kin wondered, *what will they look like after a race?*

He was soon to find out.

It was almost race time. Other cars were being pushed or towed by their crews from the garage to the pits. The last adjustments had been made; the fine-tuning was over. The specialized hand tools, the computer exhaust analyzers and vacuum gauges, had all been left behind in the garage. The only work in the pits would be emergency repairs, tire changes, and gas and oil.

High-speed pit stop stuff.

Outside the dark garage, in the bright sunshine, the cars looked like birds with colorful plumage, lined up along pit road.

All except one.

The Gray team's pit held one gray car, with no colors, no insignia, no trademarks, slogans, or signs.

Nothing but a number and a few decals required by NASCAR.

The mechanics, the pit crew, and the driver all wore gray.

They all looked exactly alike, with thin lips, short gray hair, and gray eyes.

Spooky! thought Kin.

"What's with these guys?" he asked Junior. "Don't they have any sponsors?"

"They do," said Junior, "but their sponsor is anonymous. I can't figure it. They always race, and they always finish, but they never finish first and they never finish last. Plus, they all look alike to me."

"You said it," said Kin.

As they entered pit road, they waved at Jeff Gordon. And Junior introduced Kin to another NASCAR driver, the legendary "Texas Terry" Labonte.

Farther down pit road, they passed the red and black Pontiac of one of Hotshoe's drivers, Steve Gregson.

Waddy stopped pushing long enough to wave. "Good luck," he called out cheerfully.

"Good luck back," replied Gregson, who was anxiously conferring with Hotshoe, hoping they had installed the right camshaft.

The Peytona team's Taurus rolled into its assigned pit, which was filled with neatly stacked tires, separated into stacks of four, right and left. Hand tools, air wrenches, and spare parts were neatly arranged alongside the two-foot-high wall that separated the pit from the infield.

Kin and Junior had arranged the pit while the rest of the crew had been working on the car in the garage.

"You fellows did a good job," Waddy said to Kin.

Kin beamed with pleasure, but his face fell when he heard Waddy's next words:

"Now you'll have to stay on the other side of the pit wall."

"Huh?" Kin was shocked.

"It's the rule," said Waddy. "Only seven crew members are allowed in the pits during the race."

"But I thought—" Kin tried to hide his disappointment. "I thought I was going to wash the windshield!"

"You are," said Waddy, handing him a long stick with a sponge on the end of it. "From up here. You and the dog both."

"Worf," said Scuffs.

"Darn," said Kin under his breath.

Kin watched enviously as the pit crew prepared for the race. They were all lean, intense men, who trained like athletes for the grueling teamwork and split-second work that would be required during the race. Kin knew he could perform as well as any of them. All he needed was a chance to show what he could do.

Waddy came back from his final visit to the men's room, just in time to stand at attention with his crew and listen to the National Anthem.

Then he said a short, silent prayer and pulled on his helmet.

Meanwhile, Junior reached through the narrow window of the Taurus and pulled out the steering wheel.

Waddy climbed into the car through the window. Junior handed him the steering wheel, and Waddy clipped it into place on the steering column.

Waddy's crew chief, Cope, fastened yellow plastic mesh over the open window. "Looks copacetic," he said. This was the crew chief's word for anything and everything that suited him.

Amazing, thought Kin as he watched. *No door, no steering wheel, not even a window to roll up and down. Up close, stock car racing is sure odd! It's almost like the Land of Oz!*

Kin had almost forgotten his hurt and disappointment in the excitement of preparing for the race.

The sky was bright blue, and the stands were filled with fans, all buzzing with anticipation. All that was missing was the race itself.

At that very minute, a voice came over the loudspeaker:

"Gentlemen, start your engines!"

SETTING THE PACE

The roar was like the sound of a thousand dinosaurs, all waking up from the dead at once.

Wow! thought Laptop as the forty starters of the Pine Gap 300 raced their engines, trying to keep the spark plugs from fouling. Forty high-compression V-8s filled the heavy summer air with a symphony of raw power.

"Yuck," said Laura, who didn't particularly like cars, and liked noise even less. "It sounds like a big old garbage disposal breaking down."

She and Laptop followed Wild Bill Wilde across the infield to the Cruisin' Classics Car Show area, where his Golden Hawk waited.

"You kids have to ride in the back seat," said Wild Bill as they got into the antique Studebaker.

Wild Bill started it up and dropped it into gear.

Pulling out onto the track, the sleek old Golden Hawk accelerated smoothly into the first turn.

The engine made a low rumbling growl.

The tires hummed on the rough asphalt.

"It's bumpy!" said Laptop.

"Sure enough is!" said Wild Bill. "Some of these old tracks are rougher than a cob. People think a race track is like a superhighway, but when you actually drive on it you can feel just how rough it is. Take this Pine Gap track, for instance. It started out as a dirt track, then they added on asphalt."

"It must be hard on tires," said Laura. She grimaced, thinking of the rough surface scraping away at the soft rubber.

"This track eats tires like candy," said Wild Bill.

"Look!" said Laptop. He was looking out the back window.

One by one, the race cars were pulling out of the pit road onto the track.

They fell in behind the Studebaker, two by two. The mighty roar of engines got louder and louder as more cars pulled onto the track and settled into their qualifying positions—the slower cars moving aside to allow the faster ones to take their positions in the front of the pack.

"Awesome!" breathed Laptop, lifting his computer onto the back of the seat, as if he wanted it to be able to see what he saw out the rear window of the pace car.

From the front, the race cars looked like garishly colored jungle animals, straining at their leashes, eager to be set free.

The cars were swerving from side to side: right, left, right, left.

"Can't they steer?" Laura asked.

"They are scrubbing their tires," said Wild Bill. "That warms up the rubber so the tires will grip better when the race begins."

Once, then once again, the pace car went around the track, with forty race cars following, two by two.

Wild Bill maintained a steady speed—40 miles per hour.

"Can't this old Studebaker go any faster?" Laptop asked.

Wild Bill looked hurt. "It can and will," he said. "But first I have to let the cars clock their pit road speed."

"What's that?" asked Laura.

"It's a NASCAR safety regulation," said Wild Bill. "At this track, the top speed allowed on the pit road is 40 miles per hour. Since race cars don't have speedometers, they have to follow me and note what their tachometers read when I go 40."

"I get it," said Laura. "The tachometer is the thingy that tells how fast the engine is going."

"Like this *thingy*," said Wild Bill, tapping the tachometer on the dashboard of the Golden Hawk. "It reads 1800 rpm at 40 mph. Of course, each race car is going to have its own reading, depending on the gearing."

"How can they drive without speedometers?" Laptop asked. "It seems like that would take all the fun out of racing."

"Not hardly!" said Wild Bill. "All a driver really needs to know is if he's going faster than the other guy."

"Other car, you mean," said Laura. "They're not *all* guys, are they?"

"Well, actually, at this point . . ." Wild Bill stammered. "Though, of course, there is always room for women to get into racing! Why not you?"

"No way!" said Laura. "Race cars are too noisy. Plus, I don't even like to go fast."

* * * * *

The Studebaker came out of the backstretch turn and entered the long straightaway.

Wild Bill held the speed steady at 40.

It seemed as if the track smoothed out as the Golden Hawk cruised past the stands.

The steep turns seemed almost flat. The skid marks on the asphalt wove in and out as the car passed swiftly over them. They seemed to be spiraling, like the parachutists earlier.

The smooth roar of the venerable Studebaker Golden Hawk was drowned out by the mighty snarl of forty full-bore racing engines, following right behind.

In the distance, at the end of the long straightaway, a man in a NASCAR official's uniform stood on a narrow platform overlooking the track.

He was holding a green flag, with one hand on the pole and the other on the bright green cloth.

He lifted the green flag over his head.

"Hang on, kids!" Wild Bill said. "Here's where we let them go!"

He angled to the left, toward the opening of the pit road. The pace car was out of the way!

35

The official at the start/finish line was waving the flag wildly, whipping it from side to side.

Laptop and Laura watched as the race cars sprang to life, passing them at well over 100 miles per hour already.

The roar was deafening.

The mighty snarl of the engines was mixed with the excited roar of the crowd, as the race began.

"Awesome . . ." said Laptop.

The race was on!

NOTHIN' SERIOUS

The green flag whipped through the Tennessee mountain air.

The crowd in the grandstand roared with pleasure and anticipation as forty expert and eager drivers put the accelerators of forty perfectly prepared race cars to the floor.

The Pine Gap Raceway throbbed with sound as forty drivers jockeyed for position.

Waddy Peytona's Taurus, starting in pole position, lost the lead immediately as two cars passed him on the inside.

One of them was Jeff Gordon's Chevy.

The other was Terry Labonte's Chevy.

Waddy wasn't worried. It was a long race, and he didn't expect to lead all the way.

All he had to do was stay in the top five, the front-running pack of cars. That way he could please his potential sponsor, and be ready to make his move in the last few laps of the race.

Meanwhile, he didn't want to push his Ford too hard, not until he knew how well it was running.

He stayed in third place for three laps, then four, then five.

The lead car flashed through the steep first and second turns, diving low and coming out high, almost on the wall. Waddy followed right behind. He knew from long experience that he could drive close to the wall and a cushion of air would hold him off.

The third turn, leading to the long straightaway, was more complex. Should he go high, following Jeff Gordon? Or should he take the turn lower down, where the asphalt was rougher but the turn was shorter?

Every car on the track was looking for the same thing: the groove—the route through the curves that matched perfectly with the speed, the suspension, the weather, and the driver's skill.

Even though Waddy had driven Pine Gap many times, the groove was always a little different, depending on the temperature, the other cars in the field, and whatever changes the track had undergone over the winter.

It was these little differences that Waddy was trying to discover, as he drove the first twenty laps with grim concentration.

Finally he found what seemed to be his fastest route: low on the first turn; a little higher on the second; then flat out on the short straightaway, hitting the brakes at the last instant before diving low into the last turn and coming out high for the long straightaway.

The cushion of air held the car just inches off the wall as Waddy blasted down the straightaway toward the finish line at almost a hundred and sixty miles per hour.

"Found it!" Waddy said into his radio. "I'm in the groove!"

"Copacetic!" said Cope. "You're looking fine."

Waddy could barely hear Cope's answer. He was running side by side with Gregson's red and black Pontiac.

Waddy held his position, delaying his braking just long enough to see Gregson fall back one spot.

Now Waddy was running third!

After ten more laps he was still running strong, when the crew chief came back on the radio.

"Waddy, you're copacetic!" he said. "This sponsor is going to love us."

"Knock on wood," said Waddy.

The Taurus felt just right. The engine was smooth and loud and eager, never missing a lick.

But something was wrong.

The temperature gauge was creeping up. Nothing serious, Waddy thought.

Or was it?

GOLDEN OLDIES

Bouncing slowly across the rough grass, Wild Bill Wilde pulled the Golden Hawk back into the roped-off Cruisin' Classics Car Show area.

He waved at the security guard and shut off the engine.

"That's it, kids," he said, lighting a cigar. "I have to head up to the grandstand. I'm expected in the peace officers' VIP box. You kids are welcome to come along. It's a great place to watch the race from, and I'm sure your grandpa wouldn't mind."

"No thanks," said Laura. She wrinkled her nose, trying to shut out the smell of the cigar. "I promised Infield Annie I would help her with the lunch crowd."

"And I like it here in the infield," said Laptop.

They all three got out of the car.

"Suit yourselves," said Wild Bill. And with a wave, he was off.

"Wait a minute!" Laura called after him. "Aren't you going to lock your car?"

"Nah!" Wild Bill shrugged. "It's a fact, there have been some mighty mysterious disappearances of classic cars lately. Theory is, there's a car-theft ring specializing in classics. But I'm not worried."

"Why not?" Laptop asked.

"Three reasons," said Wild Bill. He pointed toward the security guard who was sitting on a folding chair by the rope, playing a handheld video game.

"One: We have security," said Wild Bill.

Then he reached into his shirt pocket and pulled out a badge. "Two: Who's going to steal the sheriff's car?"

Then he waved his arm around at the track and the grandstand, which was already filled with racing fans. "And three: How could anybody possibly steal a car out of the infield, with thousands of people watching?"

Then he disappeared into the pedestrians-only tunnel that led from the infield to the grandstand.

* * * * *

It was too early for Laura to go to Annie's, so she and her little brother walked across the grass to the infield fence and found a spot where they could watch the race.

Laptop noticed that many of the people standing along the fence were holding electronic devices that looked like video games.

Some of them were wearing headphones and earphones.

"What's that?" Laptop asked the man next to him.

"Huh?" The man looked up, puzzled. Then he smiled and took off his earphones.

"Huh?"

"I said, what's that?" Laptop asked again, pointing at the device in the man's hand.

"Oh, that's a scanner," the man said. He held out the earphones. "Here, try it."

Laptop put his ear to one of the earphones. Laura bent down and put her ear to the other.

They both heard a storm of static. Behind the static, they could hear dim voices:

"That's better, just keep . . . "

"Don't pull out too soon, there's oil on the track . . . "

"Sounds like a bad rocker arm . . . "

"This clutch is . . . "

Laptop saw that the stranger was spinning the dial of the scanner. He pulled the earphone away from his ear.

"Scanner's the thing!" said the man with a grin. "You can listen in on the conversations between the drivers and their crew chiefs and spotters."

"What are spotters?" asked Laura, straightening up.

"Up there." The man pointed toward the roof of the control tower. "Every crew has a man up high watching the track for trouble. He's called a spotter."

"Awesome," said Laptop. "Where can I get one?"

"You can rent yourself a scanner over at the grandstand," said the man.

"How much?" asked Laura.

"Oh, about twenty bucks or so."

Laptop groaned.

Laura laughed. "Thanks," she said, handing the man his earphones back. "We could never afford that!"

"I thought you were going to watch the race," Laura said.

She stood at the fence. Laptop sat on the ground beside her, concentrating on his computer.

"Laptop, please!" she insisted. "You can't spend your whole life playing stupid computer games."

"I'm not playing games," Laptop said.

"What are you doing, then?"

"Making us a scanner. I think."

"How?" Laura sat down beside him.

The Travis kids' father had been a computer designer. The Apricot 07 was his last and most advanced design.

"Dad left a lot of strange programs on this machine," said Laptop. "Most of them were betas, or experimental designs. I know the Apricot had a GPS— a global positioning satellite—transponder, a permanent hookup to the atomic clock in Washington, a weather channel and storm warning center; plus a built-in FM receiver . . ."

"Whoa!" said Laura. "What are you talking about?"

"This," said Laptop. He showed her the icon for a program called CyberHam. "Maybe with a little tweaking to take in shortwave frequencies . . ."

While his sister watched, amazed, Laptop went into the Apricot's system file and adjusted the FM frequencies. He followed his instincts. So far, they had proven to be pretty good. Laptop seemed to understand software and computers instinctively, the way dogs understood how to hunt, or fish understand how to swim.

The people who noticed him sitting on the grass, totally absorbed in his machine, humming to himself and rocking back and forth, thought he was playing a computer game.

Which, in a way, he was.

Suddenly a voice came through the computer's tiny twin speakers:

". . . loose as a goose in the rear . . . "

". . . that right tire a little low . . . "

Success! Laptop was on the air with his own improvised scanner!

He found a menu to change channels, and searched through the frequencies until he heard a familiar voice:

". . . how in the world could it be heating up? . . . "

It was Cope, Waddy Peytona's crew chief!

"I'm telling you . . ." said Waddy. His voice was crackling with static and something that sounded a lot like worry.

Laptop stood up and looked through the fence again. The cars flashed past so fast that they were just blurs. He couldn't tell which car was which.

He sat back down beside his computer. It was more fun to listen than to watch. The Apricot 07 made a good scanner. The problem was, he didn't have any earphones.

And with the cars rushing past only a few feet away . . .

VVVVRRRROOOOOM!

VVVVRRRROOOOOM!

VVVVRRRROOOOOM!

It was hard to hear!

RIDING THE BULL

The race went on for twenty, then thirty, then forty laps.

The first cars were beginning to come into the pits.

Gas tanks needed to be topped off, and tires needed to be changed.

Waddy Peytona's Taurus was the sixth car to come in.

He lost third place by pitting, but he knew he could make it up.

He pulled onto the pit road at a steady 40 mph, then screeched to a halt in his team's pit.

The jack man lifted the car.

Junior and the other tire changer leapt into action. The air wrench whined, and almost as soon as the wheels were off the ground, the tires were off and changed.

Meanwhile, at the back of the car, the tank was

being filled from a giant gas can held by one man, while the other man caught the overflow.

Kin wasn't just watching all this. He had his own job to do. And though it wasn't exactly glamorous or exciting, it was still crucial.

Since he couldn't be in the pit, according to NASCAR regulations, he reached over with his long stick and washed the windshield with the sponge attached to the end.

So far the race was going well, but Waddy was worried.

"The engine is heating up just a little," he said. "The temperature is rising lap by lap. It's not a problem yet, but . . . "

Cope listened to the idling engine. Waddy raced it a couple of times.

Everything sounded fine. There was no time to look under the hood.

"Sounds copacetic to me," said Cope. "Just push on and hope for the best," he said.

The car came down off its jack after twenty seconds.

Waddy slammed it into gear, released the clutch, and roared off.

Waddy was in sixth place now, but he would soon be back in third—if the tires held up, if the engine held up, if nobody cut him off or ran into him.

Driving a race car was like riding a wild bull—it required a complex and rare combination of genius, art, science, luck.

And hope, thought Waddy as he brought the Taurus up to speed and joined the rest of the pack on the straightaway. *I'll do what Cope suggested: I'll hope for the best!*

PROMISE? PROMISE!

Laura was bored.

The race had been exciting for a while, but watching the cars whip through the turns was losing its appeal.

Laura looked at her watch.

One o'clock already.

It was time to head for Infield Annie's.

"Laptop, come with me," she said. Her little brother was sitting on the ground by the fence, listening to the crews and the drivers on his computer/scanner.

"No way!" Laptop said. He wanted to watch the race, or at least listen to the race, and he definitely didn't want to hang out at Infield Annie's and smell the greens and corn bread.

"I'll stay here," he said.

"Promise?"

"Promise."

"Well . . . okay," said Laura.

She looked around. There was a crowd along the fence watching the race. A few people were walking around inside the roped-off Cruisin' Classics Golden Oldies Car Show area.

The security guard was playing his video game.

"Okay," said Laura, patting her brother on the head and walking off toward Infield Annie's. "I guess nothing can go wrong here in the infield."

How wrong can a girl be?

Laptop was bored.

He wanted to hear the drivers talking, but the sound of the cars was drowning them out. He wished he had some earphones.

He turned away from the infield fence, where the cars were roaring past in a deafening blur, and looked behind him, toward the car show area.

The show was almost deserted. Only two people were inside the roped-off area, a man and a woman.

The woman had a ponytail. She wore a wide, twirly skirt with felt poodles sewn to it. She looked like a 1950s bobby-soxer.

The man had long hair in an Elvis-style ducktail. He wore his shirt collar turned up, and his jeans were tight, 1950s style. He carried a canvas bag.

They must be part of the show, Laptop thought.

The cars gleamed in the sun. The Golden Hawk was the shiniest and prettiest of them all.

And, Laptop remembered, it was unlocked!

With his computer tucked under his arm, Laptop walked away from the fence and into the car show area.

The security guard looked up from his handheld video game.

"Hi," Laptop said.

"Hi," said the guard.

"I'm a friend of Mr. Wilde's," said Laptop.

"Whatever," said the guard. "Just don't be touching the cars."

"Oh, I won't," said Laptop.

Laptop waited until the man and woman weren't looking his way, and walked over to the Studebaker. He pretended to be admiring it.

He waited until the guard was engrossed in his game before he opened the door of the Studebaker.

The rear seat looked so inviting!

He got in and quietly closed the door behind him.

With the car windows rolled up, it was easy to hear the voices on the computer/scanner.

He lay down on the seat so nobody could see him, and scanned around on the frequencies until he found Waddy and Cope.

They were still talking about the race car over-heating. Waddy had fallen back to seventh place.

That's bad, Laptop thought. *He has to place at least fifth to get a sponsor.*

Through the glass the cars were a distant buzzing.

Laptop lay back on the seat and listened. He closed his eyes. The world outside the car faded into a dream . . .

SING ME A SONG!

"Where's what's-his-name, your little brother, Ragtop?" asked Infield Annie.

"You mean Laptop," said Laura. Grown-ups never got names right, not even nicknames; especially nicknames. "He's watching the race."

"As long as he doesn't get lost."

"He's older than he looks," said Laura. "He's almost eight. There's no way for him to get lost, or seriously lost, here in the infield. So I came over here to help you out."

She ducked behind Annie's counter and began to tie on an apron.

"Hold it, girl," said Annie. She untied Laura's apron and handed her the Wabash Cannonball guitar she had inherited from her mother.

"You'd just get in the way back here behind the counter," said Annie. "The help I need from you is the same help I got yesterday—I need you to sing a song and bring in some customers."

"You already have customers," said Laura.

True enough. Even though it wasn't yet noon, people were already waiting in line for Annie's famous corn bread and beans.

"Then I need you to keep them happy," said Annie. "I don't want them to get impatient, waiting for my beans to get ready."

She lifted the lid of an enormous pot and sniffed.

The sweet smell of red beans and ham hocks wafted through the air.

"Sing the folks a song, Laura. It'll do the folks good and, who knows, it might do you good, too. I know it'll do me good."

Laura took the little guitar out of the case.

A mother-of-pearl inlay around the sound hole showed an old-fashioned steam train rounding a mountain curve.

More pearl inlays were on the neck.

Laura held the sound hole up to her ear and gently brushed her fingers across the strings.

It sounded okay. But how could she be sure? Laura didn't know how to tune a guitar—much less play one! But last night, when she had picked up the Wabash, her fingers had somehow "remembered" how to play it.

It was almost like magic. Was it because it had been her mother's guitar?

It was still a mystery.

"Up here," said Annie. She patted the counter.

Using a stool for a step, Laura climbed up and sat down on the counter, overlooking the infield.

Five or six friendly faces broke into smiles. The people waiting in line seemed to want to hear her sing.

Laura wondered if they, or anyone, would be able to hear her over the roar of forty race cars.

And would she even be able to play? What if the magic had worn off?

Tentatively she put the guitar across her lap.

The fingers of her left hand curled around the neck and found the strings. Their bite felt familiar.

— — — — — — — — — — — — — —

Her right hand was tingling as it strummed a chord, then another.

The sound was bright and high.

Tentatively at first, then a little louder, Laura Travis began to sing . . .

BRAIN LOCK

Laptop lay dreaming, curled in the back seat of Wild Bill Wilde's classic Studebaker Golden Hawk.

The security guard didn't know he was there.

He looked up from his handheld video game and saw a couple approaching him.

The woman had a ponytail. She was wearing a wide, twirly skirt with felt poodles sewn to it. She looked like a 1950s bobby-soxer.

The man with her wore his long hair in an Elvis-style ducktail. His shirt collar was turned up, and his jeans were tight, 1950s style.

They must be part of the show, thought the security guard.

"Can I help you?" he asked.

"You sure can," said the woman. "Can you tell me which one of these cars is the most valuable?"

"That's easy," said the guard. He set down his video game and pointed to the Studebaker. "That's a Golden Hawk. It was the pace car."

He looked up at the woman curiously.

"But I figured you would know. Aren't you part of the show?"

"Not exactly," said the woman.

The security guard didn't notice that the man was replacing his video game with another one that looked just like it.

(He was not a very attentive security guard.)

"Thanks," said the couple, and they walked on.

The guard picked up his video game.

He punched PLAY.

Weird! he thought. *The display is all a wrong . . .*

That was his first and last thought for the day. Suddenly his eyes went glassy, and he fell into a trance.

The 1950s man nodded at the woman. The 1950s woman winked at the man.

Step one of their plan had worked. The guard had been hypnotized by their special secret digital-strobe brain lock video game!

Locked in a trance, the security guard stared at the tiny screen.

The man and the woman stepped into the roped-off Cruisin' Classics Golden Oldies area.

Walking casually but deliberately, they crossed to the Golden Hawk.

While the woman scanned the crowd to make sure no one was watching, the man opened his canvas bag. He took out a thick rope with a huge plastic hook on one end.

He quickly wrapped the rope around and under the car, so that the big hook was on top of the roof.

Meanwhile, the woman opened her compact and fixed her lipstick.

The mirror in her compact flashed in the sun.

On the distant top of Rockcastle Mountain, a mirror flashed back.

A huge shape appeared from behind a nearby hill, and began to move slowly through the air toward the race track.

It was a silver blimp—with a scarlet lightning bolt on the side!

HEATING UP

Kin had never worked so hard in his life.

Even though he was not in the pit, he was kept busy filling gas cans, getting soda for the pit crew, washing the windshield whenever Waddy's car came in, and generally feeling with every heartbeat the tremendous tension and excitement of NASCAR racing.

And he loved it!

He tried to hide his smile, though. It seemed disloyal to be having so much fun when Waddy Peytona was losing.

He had never regained his third position.

In fact, he had dropped back to seventh.

Cope was on the radio with Waddy nonstop, his thin face was creased with worry. "Everything was copacetic," he said. "I can't figure what went wrong!"

The Taurus was overheating. Not enough to take it out of the race, but just enough to keep it from passing the other cars.

Waddy could barely hold his position—and he was gradually slipping back.

"Worf worf," said Scuffs, scurrying after Kin.

Scuffs was happy, too. He had finally found a family, and what did he care who won the race?

"Worf!"

"Sssshhh!" said Kin. He knelt down and wagged his finger in the dog's face. "Quit acting so darn cheerful. It annoys people."

Wild Bill was enjoying the race.

He was sitting with his old friend, State Trooper Terence Thom, in the peace officers' VIP box. From the box, they could see the entire track, and the infield, too.

The race was two-thirds over. Steve Gregson and Jeff Gordon were battling for the lead.

Waddy was not doing as well as expected. He was in seventh—no, eighth—place, as the Gray Brothers car passed him on the short straightaway.

- - - - - - - - - - - - - - - -

Wonder what's wrong? Wild Bill tuned his scanner up and down, looking for Waddy's frequency. Maybe if he could listen in to Waddy and Cope he could figure it out.

"That's odd," said Trooper Thom. He handed Wild Bill his binoculars. "Check out the car show."

Wild Bill put the binoculars to his eyes and looked into the infield.

There was his Golden Hawk, under the Cruisin' Classics banner. What a gorgeous car!

But why was that strange man tying a rope around it?

And who was that strange woman with the flashing mirror compact?

"What are they doing to your car?" asked Trooper Thom.

"Beats me," said Wild Bill. "But I don't like it. And now the woman is taking her clothes off!"

"Let me see," said Trooper Thom, reaching for his binoculars.

"In a minute," said Wild Bill.

While he watched through the binoculars, the woman and the man both stepped out of their 1950s outfits. Underneath, they wore identical silver spandex tights decorated with scarlet lightning bolts.

"Now they're taking off their wigs," said Wild Bill.

"Let me see," said Trooper Thom.

"In a minute," said Wild Bill. "Now they're opening a canvas bag. It looks like it has a couple of parachutes in it. They're stuffing the clothes in the bag and zipping it up."

"Let me see," said Trooper Thom.

"In a minute," said Wild Bill. "Now they're putting the bag in the trunk of my car! And—what's that noise?"

There was a buzzing noise overhead, louder than the race cars on the track.

Wild Bill looked up.

A huge silver blimp was crossing the grandstand!

Wild Bill handed the binoculars back to Trooper Thom and watched in amazement as the blimp motored slowly across the race track toward the infield.

All the faces in the grandstand were turned upward.

"Must be part of the air show," said Trooper Thom.

"I . . . don't think so," said Wild Bill.

He was getting a strange, uneasy feeling.

It got worse as the blimp stopped and hovered

over the Cruisin' Classics Golden Oldies Car Show.

It got even worse as a hook dropped from the blimp, and the man and woman attached it to the rope wrapped around the Golden Hawk.

It got still worse as the blimp picked the car up!

"Hey!" said Wild Bill.

The man and woman scampered up the rope toward the blimp. They were as agile as squirrels.

"Hey!" said Wild Bill. "That's my car!"

"You sure that's not part of the air show?" asked Trooper Thom, as the blimp rose higher and higher, with the car dangling underneath it.

"Darn right I'm sure!" said Wild Bill.

A door opened in the bottom of the gondola slung under the blimp. The man and the woman disappeared inside.

"Call the police!" said Wild Bill.

"I *am* the police," said Trooper Thom. "So are you. You're the sheriff, remember?"

"Then we've got to do something," said Wild Bill as the blimp motored slowly off on the direction of Rockcastle Mountain. "Because someone has stolen my car!"

FLIGHT OF THE GOLDEN HAWK

Laptop dreamed he was flying.

Flying in a golden airplane!

It was finned like a fish, gently rocking back and forth, sailing through the clouds.

He smiled and opened one eye.

The only problem with dreams was that they always went away when you woke up.

This one was pretty persistent, though.

Laptop still felt like he was flying.

He was still rocking gently back and forth.

And there, out the window, was a cloud!

He remembered where he was. He was in the back seat of a car—Wild Bill's Studebaker. His computer was beside him on the seat.

But something was wrong. The light was weird,

and—yes! That was a cloud that had just floated by the window.

Laptop opened his other eye.

He sat up and looked out the window of the car.

What he saw made him want to throw up!

Not that it was disgusting. It was quite beautiful: rolling hills, trees, and green fields. The problem was, it was thousands of feet straight down!

And the car was swinging back and forth like the seat on a Ferris wheel.

In the distance, Laptop could see the Pine Gap Raceway. From here it looked like a slot-car track.

He rolled down the window, leaned out, and looked up.

There was the silver blimp with the scarlet lightning bolt on the side.

The car was hanging from it by a rope.

"Yikes!" Laptop said to himself.

The air show was still going on, and the Golden Hawk was part of it.

And now he was, too!

How can I get out of here? Laptop wondered.

He looked down. It was too late to jump, that was for sure!

He had to let someone know what had happened. He had to get help.

But how?

Then his eyes lit on his computer, his Apricot 07. It had "gone to sleep," automatically, as it always did when he wasn't using it.

Laptop "woke" it by hitting a key. It was already running the CyberHam radio scanner program.

He started scanning through the channels.

TEAMWORK IS EVERYTHING

"Did you see that blimp and that flying car?" Junior asked. "I think they ought to hold off on the air show stuff until the race is over."

"Me too," said Kin. "It makes it hard to concentrate!"

Kin was trying his best, but he felt like he needed five hands to do his job.

One for the stick, one for the dog, one for the squeegee, one for the soap solution . . .

And one just to keep count!

With one hand he held the stick at the ready, so that he could reach over the wall and wash the windshield when Waddy made his last pit stop.

With the other he was helping Junior replace an air hose on the air wrench he would use to quickly replace two tires on the next and last pit stop.

If he had another hand, he would use it to pat Scuffs, who was patiently waiting by the pit wall.

"Worf," said Scuffs.

"You said it," said Kin.

The Pine Gap 300 was three-fourths over. The Waddy Peytona pit, like the others up and down pit road, was a picture of controlled chaos and carefully coordinated confusion.

Men scrambled everywhere, filling gas cans, stacking tires, replacing spare parts—all getting ready for the next pit stop that would decide the race.

Fast, efficient pit stops are the key to racing success. In many ways the pit crews are the unsung heroes of auto racing. They must be able to refuel, repair, and re-tire a hundred-thousand-dollar race car in twenty seconds or less, and do it several times in every race.

Kin Travis could think of no greater honor than to be a member of a pit crew—unless it was to be a driver.

But where would he ever find enough hands?

"Here, kid, hold this darn thing!"

Now, to make things worse, he was supposed to hold Cope's radio while the crew chief searched through a spare toolbox for a can of radiator sealer that he hoped might fix Waddy's overheating problem on his next pit stop.

"Think it'll help?" Kin asked.

"Heck no! I want to have it ready, just in case," said Cope. "Even though I don't think a leak is the problem."

Whatever the problem was, it was costing Waddy the race. With his engine weakened by overheating, he had fallen back to ninth place. And he had to finish in the top five if he wanted to get a sponsor.

Over the radio, Kin could hear Waddy and his spotter strategizing. A pit stop always cost two or three positions in the race. Waddy couldn't afford to let any more cars get in front of him.

"I'll keep going and hope for a caution!" he said. A caution flag meant no passing. It was the best time for all the drivers to pit, since they wouldn't lose their spots, on the way in at least. Where they would be on the way out would be up to their teams.

But what if there wasn't a caution? The yellow flag only came out when there was an accident or a problem on the track.

Hoping for the best sometimes meant hoping for the worst. Kin was amazed by the intricacies of racing. He had thought that speed was everything. Now he saw that strategy and planning were just as important. It was teamwork that won the races. A driver and his crew were a team, just like the pitcher and the fielders on a baseball team.

Racing was no one-man show.

The crackling voices of Waddy and the spotter were interrupted by a new voice.

It was a familiar voice, but not one Kin had expected to hear on the radio.

"Somebody help me!"

It was Laptop.

Cope heard and looked up, confused. So did Junior.

Kin put the earphones on.

"Help! Junior, Cope, Mr. Peytona, somebody. Tell Kin and Grandpa Hotshoe. I'm in the car the blimp is lifting, the Golden Hawk! The air show people must not know I'm here!"

Kin, Junior, and Cope all looked up at once. Just in time to see the blimp, with the car dangling beneath it, disappear into a fluffy white cloud!

LIKE RIDING A BICYCLE

"That's my car," said Wild Bill.

He was standing with his friend, State Trooper Thom, in the peace officers' VIP box of the Pine Gap Raceway.

Far above them, the blimp with the Golden Hawk hanging beneath it was sailing toward Rockcastle Mountain.

"Are you sure it's not part of the air show?" asked Trooper Thom one last time.

"Of course I'm sure!" said Wild Bill. "Do you think I'd give anyone permission to pick up my Studebaker classic and dangle it under a blimp like a trout on a line? It's an aerial car-napping! Call the Air Force."

"I'm not sure we should," said Trooper Thom. "Most people think it's part of the air show. We don't want to stop the race and start a panic. What if the thieves drop the car on the grandstand and run away?"

Or just drop the car! thought Wild Bill with alarm. "You're right," he said. "But what can we do?"

"I'll call headquarters and order a helicopter," said Trooper Thom.

"Good idea," said Wild Bill. "But tell them to hurry."

The silver blimp with the scarlet lightning bolt on the side was already disappearing into a cloud near the top of Rockcastle Mountain.

"And what's all the commotion down there?" asked the state trooper.

He pointed down into the grandstand. A young man was running up the steps toward the VIP booth, taking two steps at a time. An older man in a "gimme" hat was right behind him.

"That's Hotshoe Hunter and his grandson, Kin," said Wild Bill, puzzled. "It looks like they've got some kind of problem of their own. They're all hot and bothered about something!"

I wonder if Laptop sees that? Laura wondered.

While she sang, she looked up. The silver blimp with the scarlet lightning bolt was now thousands of feet above the race track, motoring steadily toward the rocky ridge of Rockcastle Mountain.

Below it dangled the Studebaker Golden Hawk— the pace car Laura and Laptop had ridden in.

Neat! she thought. *I hope Laptop is watching. He loves air show stuff.*

But Laura didn't have time to think about Laptop. She was busy singing for the crowd at Infield Annie's. She looked back down at her guitar and concentrated on her singing.

Well, she didn't *concentrate*, exactly. In fact, if she thought about playing the guitar, her fingers didn't know what to do. If she thought about singing, she didn't know it.

But if she just played and sang without thinking, it was easy. Her fingers knew the chords. Her voice knew the tune and the words.

It was like riding a bicycle. If she thought about it, she wobbled and fell over. If she just *did* it, it was easy.

It was puzzling, but it worked. It was almost like magic! No matter how complicated or unfamiliar the song, Laura always seemed to come up with the next verse, the next chord.

And that note must have been the last note— because she hit a chord and stopped, surprising even herself.

The tiny crowd standing in line at Infield Annie's applauded and cheered. A man in a white suit was applauding especially loudly. Laura had seen him before. He had been through the line twice.

Laura liked hearing the applause.

What's it like to do this on a real stage? she wondered.

The weird thing was, she almost knew.

She could almost feel the pleasure of standing in the lights and hearing applause and cheers.

She could almost feel the buzz of a crowd, the sound of boots on a wooden floor, the crackle of enthusiastic applause.

It was like trying to remember a dream. Somebody else's dream . . .

"That was great, honey," said Annie. "Why don't you take a little break. You deserve one."

"Sure," said Laura. She carefully put the gleaming little Wabash Cannonball guitar away in its hardshell case. "Maybe I can help you."

— — — — — — — — — — — — — — — — —

Annie shrugged. "I don't think so," she said.

Laura thought Annie was just being polite. So she tied on an apron and got behind the counter.

Laura tried to help with the cooking, flipping the corn bread "hoecakes" on the propane stove. But Annie reached over her shoulder and did it faster.

She tried to help serving, dishing greens onto a plate. But again, Annie reached over her shoulder and did it faster.

She tried to help make change, but Annie reached over her shoulder and counted out quarters with one hand while she was serving with the other.

The older woman's hands were moving so fast, they were a blur. She was like three people, one serving, one cooking, and one making change. While Laura watched, amazed, Annie was filling a plate, passing it to a customer, counting out change, stirring the stove, and asking the next customer, "What'll it be, hon?"

"I give up," said Laura, stepping out of the way. "I thought Southerners were supposed to be slow."

"That's just a rumor," said Annie. "If you think I'm fast, you ought to see the boys in the pit crews. Say, did you see the rest of the air show?"

With her big wooden spoon, she pointed up at the faraway blimp with the car dangling underneath it.

"I sure did," said Laura. "It's awesome!"

"You sound like your little brother," said Annie. "I hope he has a good spot where he can see it all."

LAPTOP'S AIR SHOW

Laptop did have a good spot—the best seat in the house.

He was in the back seat of the Golden Hawk.

After he got over his initial panic, he climbed into the front seat and sat behind the wheel. He pretended he was driving—or rather, flying—the classic Studebaker.

"This is actually kind of awesome," he said into the microphone on his computer. "I'm part of the air show!"

"Not exactly," said a gruff, worried voice.

"Grandpa Hotshoe, is that you?" Laptop asked. He had reached his grandfather and big brother, and they had gone for help. He was expecting them to call back.

"This is Wild Bill Wilde, young man. The sheriff and the owner of the purloined classic. Your granddad is here with me. And we both want you to sit tight."

"Okay, sure," said Laptop. "I'll sit tight."

What else can I do? he wondered. *Jump out?*

He looked out the window and shivered. It was a long, long way down!

Grandpa Hotshoe came on the radio. "The good news is, we're going to rescue you," he said. "As soon as we figure out a way to do it."

That doesn't sound very positive, thought Laptop. *I wonder what the bad news is.*

"The bad news is, you're not part of the air show at all. You've been kidnapped!"

"Kidnapped?" Laptop was more surprised than frightened. "Why would anybody want to kidnap me?"

"It's not you!" said Wild Bill. "It's the car. It's a carnapping! You're just along for the ride."

Kin came on the radio. "What were you doing in the car anyway?"

"Taking a nap," said Laptop. *Not that it's any of your business anyway!*

Trooper Thom came on the radio. "The car-theft ring that has been stealing classics has struck again! Everybody thinks it's part of the air show. But it's not!"

Hotshoe Hunter came back on the radio. "The

good thing is, they don't know you are inside. So just sit tight until they land, and then you can escape."

"That's right," said Wild Bill. "We've ordered a helicopter. Meanwhile, we're following you from the ground. As long as they don't know you're there, you're okay."

Kin came on the radio. "What if they are listening in?"

"Huh?" asked Wild Bill, Hotshoe, and Trooper Thom, all at once.

But Laptop knew what his brother was talking about. "They can hear us on a scanner," he said.

"The boys are right," said Hotshoe. "They can pick it up—just like we picked it up."

"Ooops! We'd better quit talking on this frequency!" said Trooper Thom.

"Too late," said Laptop.

"What do you mean?" asked Hotshoe, Wild Bill, and Trooper Thom, all at the same time.

"They've already been listening in," said Laptop.

"How do you know?" Kin asked.

"Because," said Laptop, "I can see a man and the woman above me. They're the same two who parachuted from the blimp earlier. They just opened a door in the blimp. They are looking down toward the car. And they both have guns. And knives, too!"

AIR PIRATES

Laptop rolled down the right front window of the Golden Hawk.

He leaned out to take another look.

Maybe it had all been a dream—or a nightmare.

But no, it was real. He was three thousand feet in the air, sailing slowly over the wooded ridges of East Tennessee. Far behind, the Pine Gap Raceway looked like a slot-car track.

He looked up. The silver blimp sailed through wispy clouds. The door was still open, but the man and the woman were gone.

No, not gone.

They were climbing down the rope.

Descending swiftly hand over hand, two athletic figures in skintight Lycra suits.

Both wore Uzi submachine guns slung over their backs.

Both carried long, curved knives in their teeth.

"What am I gonna do?" Laptop wondered out loud.

"Don't panic," said Trooper Thom.

"That's a big help!" said Laptop. "There are two killers, or car thieves at least, climbing down a rope toward me. I'm trapped three thousand feet in the air, and you're telling me not to panic."

"Don't get smart with your elders, boy," said Hotshoe.

"Sorry," said Laptop. "But I am a little worried. They're getting closer."

"If you had a gun, you could shoot the rope in two," mused Wild Bill. "But then the car would fall."

And me with it, thought Laptop. *Who does the thinking for grown-ups?*

Kin came on the radio. "You said they parachuted down earlier, Laptop. Are they wearing parachutes now?"

"No."

"Could they have put their parachutes in the car?" asked Kin.

"I saw them put a bag in the trunk!" said Wild Bill.

"Is there any way to get into the trunk from the back seat?" asked Kin.

"The seat cushion pulls out," said Wild Bill. "Then if you reach through . . . Laptop, are you there? Can you hear me? I have an idea."

"I'm here," said Laptop. He was way ahead of Wild Bill. He was already in the back seat. He had pulled the seat cushion out, and was reaching through the crack, into the darkness.

He felt a canvas nag. He found the handle and pulled.

A bag came through the crack.

He unzipped it.

Out poured a woman's dress, a man's suit, two wigs, sunglasses . . . and two parachutes!

"Just a minute," said Hotshoe, his voice tiny over the computer/scanner's speakers. "I'm not sure I like this parachute idea."

"What else is there?" Laptop asked as he straightened out the harness of the parachute.

There were two straps for his legs, making the harness into a kind of a seat. Two more straps for his arms.

The parachute itself was in a square bag that

strapped against his chest, like a backwards back-pack.

Could this be right? Laptop wondered.

It seemed reversed. It felt awkward.

A cord with a ring on the end of it dangled from the square bag. *The rip cord?*

"I don't like this parachute idea," said Hotshoe over the computer/scanner. "You're just a kid, you don't know how to use a parachute."

I guess I could wait and ask them for instructions, Laptop thought wryly, looking out the window and up.

The man and woman were only yards away.

"Let's reconsider this parachute business," said Wild Bill.

"Laptop, can you hear me?" asked Kin.

"Yeah."

"I'm looking through the binoculars. The two bandits are almost to the car. You don't have any time to waste. Can you get the chute strapped on okay?"

"Yes," said Laptop. *I hope.*

"Good. Now, can you find the rip cord?"

"Yes," said Laptop. *I hope.*

- - - - - - - - - - - - - - - - -

"Then just go. Don't look down and think about it. Open the door and roll out. Count to five and pull the cord. Okay?"

"Okay," said Laptop.

He turned off his Apricot 07 computer. He closed it and clutched it to his chest.

He could hear footsteps on the roof of the car.

He climbed into the front seat and opened the door of the car.

He couldn't help looking down.

The race track was a tiny dot. The mountains were like wrinkles in a rug.

Laptop's stomach churned. It was too far! It was too scary! He couldn't do it!

Then he felt something brush the back of his leg.

He looked up and saw a hand reaching in through the car window on the other side.

Laptop closed his eyes and whispered, "Geronimo."

He rolled out the door, into the sky.

He fell, spinning . . . and then remembered what Kin had said. He clutched the ring on the rip cord and counted:

"One . . . "
"Two . . . "
"Three . . . "
"Four . . . "
"Five!"
He pulled the rip cord.
Nothing happened.

PULL THE RIP CORD!

The Pine Gap 300 was on its last twenty laps.

The roar of the cars was as loud as ever, but Laura wasn't paying attention to them. She was busy performing—and enjoying it.

Laura had learned the first lesson of show business.

You can't sing to a crowd. A singer always performs best for one person.

The greatest singers are those who have learned to pick out one sympathetic face in a crowd, and direct their heart and soul toward that one individual. It adds intensity and personality to a performance.

That's exactly what Laura was doing. She was singing not to everyone in line at Infield Annie's, but to one man who seemed more interested, more sympathetic, than the others.

In fact, he was so interested and sympathetic that he had been back several times for more beans and corn bread. And, Laura assumed, to hear her sing.

He wore a white suit and a cowboy hat, and he carried a shiny alligator briefcase.

"Will you miss me when I'm gone?" Laura sang. It was an old Carter family classic, and though she had never heard it before—at least, as far as she knew—the words sprang to her mouth just as the chords seemed to spring to her fingertips.

When she finished the song, the people in line applauded politely. But the man in the white suit whistled and cheered.

I already have one fan, Laura thought.

Or was that her imagination?

She blushed and set down her gleaming little Wabash guitar.

"Look!" said Infield Annie from behind the counter. "More air show!"

Laura looked upward. There, far above, was the blimp with the car dangling underneath it. As she watched, the car door opened and a tiny figure tumbled out.

Pretty spectacular, Laura thought. *Sort of a car show and an air show put together. And now, more parachutists!*

"Ooooooh!" said the people standing in line as they watched the parachutist fall, farther and farther.

"Oooooh!" said Laura. She hoped Laptop was watching. He loved this kind of daredevil stuff.

But why didn't the parachute open?

"What's he doing?" asked Hotshoe.

"What's he doing?" asked Wild Bill and Trooper Thom together.

"What do you think he's doing? He's jumping!" said Kin.

Looking up, he saw his little brother, just a tiny dot falling through the immense blue sky.

The car bandits were getting into the Golden Hawk just as Laptop was tumbling out. The blimp with the car underneath it was just about to disappear over the crest of Rockcastle Mountain.

"Good kid! I guess he got the parachute out of the trunk!" said Wild Bill.

"Smart kid! I guess he managed to get it on!" said Hotshoe.

"Brave kid! Now I hope he can figure out how to work it," said Trooper Thom.

"I'm sure he will," said Kin. He had the smartest little brother in the world. (Even if he was the most aggravating, sometimes.)

But Kin's confidence began to fade as he watched the tiny dot that was Laptop tumble toward the earth, falling free, farther and farther.

He must have counted to five, Kin thought. *He could have counted to ten!*

Why wasn't the parachute opening?

METEOR ATTACK!

"Darn," said Laptop.

He pulled the rip cord again.

Nothing happened.

"Double darn," said Laptop. He wasn't supposed to curse, ever.

But this was serious.

The ground was still a long way away, but it was getting closer.

Laptop pulled the rip cord again.

Nothing.

He opened the parachute pack on his chest. Then he saw the problem.

The chute was tangled in the cords.

Meanwhile, the ground was rushing up at 100 miles per hour.

Behind him, Laptop could see the blimp, heading

straight toward the craggy top of Rockcastle Mountain.

Far below, he could see the Pine Gap Raceway.

The cars were still speeding around, fighting for position. From here, they looked almost slow.

Laptop pulled at the tangled cords.

They just tangled more.

He needed two hands. But one hand was clutching his Apricot 07, the supercomputer his father had designed just before he had been killed in the crash of World Wide 888.

He didn't want to let it go.

But he had no choice. He knew his father wouldn't want him to go *splat* against the ground like a bug against a windshield.

He had to get the parachute untangled.

Grimacing, Laptop let go of the computer.

Oddly enough, it didn't fall. It just hung there at his side. It was like pictures he had seen of astronauts in orbit. Weightless . . .

Laptop realized that since he was falling, too, he was keeping up with the Apricot 07.

Maybe he wouldn't lose his computer after all!

He began to pull at the cords in the chest pack. He ripped the tangle free, and pulled out the silk underneath it.

WHHHOOOOOOOSH!

The chest pack erupted in a storm of string and cord and fabric. It shot up past Laptop's face like smoke.

WHHAAAAAMMMM!

Laptop's arms were almost pulled out of his shoulders.

Suddenly, instead of falling, he was hanging from a rectangle of billowing silk.

He reached out, but it was too late.

His computer was just a dot, falling faster and faster toward the race track far below.

"Farewell," Laptop whispered. A tear rolled down his cheek, then dried from the wind before he could wipe it off.

There was no time to mourn. He had to figure out where, and how, he was going to land.

Laptop looked around for the blimp. He wanted to get as far away from it as possible.

No problem. The blimp wasn't going to make it over the top of Rockcastle Mountain. It was sailing directly into a cliff. Unless it pulled up . . .

Laptop closed his eyes. He didn't want to watch the explosion.

When he opened his eyes again, the blimp and the car were both gone. But there were no flames, no wreckage.

Could the blimp and the car have made it over the top? Laptop wondered. But that was impossible. It must have crashed. The debris must have fallen down the cliff, into the trees.

Besides, Laptop had other worries. He could hear the cars on the track far below. They sounded like a swarm of angry bees.

"I sure don't want to land on the race track and get run over," Laptop muttered. "Wonder if I can steer this thing?"

Then he remembered what Wild Bill had told him.

He pulled the right rope and the parachute turned to the right.

He pulled the left rope and it turned to the left.

"Awesome!" Laptop yelled out loud.

This was fun!

Pulling the ropes, he went down in a swooping spiral, aiming for the infield.

* * * * *

"Awesome," said Laura, looking up at the chute that had just opened.

Then she laughed at herself. "I sound like Laptop!" she said. "I hope he's enjoying all this from the infield fence where he's watching the race."

It was time for a few more songs.

Laura stepped out of the sun, underneath Annie's awning. She sat on top of the counter and took out her guitar.

She was just about to strike the first chord when— WHAM!

Something hit the awning, bounced off, and landed in Annie's big pot of greens.

"What was that!?!" Annie yelled. "A meteor?"

"A comet?" guessed Laura. "Don't touch it, it's probably radioactive or something!"

She could see a corner of it, sticking up out of the pot. It looked almost familiar . . .

"Oh no," said Wild Bill as the blimp with the car dangling beneath it disappeared behind a peak of Rockcastle Mountain. "My car is gone for good!"

"Too bad about your car," Hotshoe said, smiling up at the parachute spiraling down. "But at least my grandson is safe."

"Looks like he's going to land in the infield," said Kin.

The crowd in the grandstand was looking up at the tiny figure circling down. They still thought it was part of the air show.

But why weren't they watching the race?

Kin found out when Junior came racing up the steps to the VIP box, with Scuffs right behind him.

"The caution flag is out!" Junior said.

Kin was puzzled. "What does that mean?"

"It means we need you back in the pit. Dad will be coming in for his last pit stop."

Kin looked up at the tiny figure parachuting down under the parachute. Then he looked at his grandfather . . .

Who nodded.

"I'll head for the infield and catch up with Laptop," Hotshoe said. "You go and help Waddy and his crew. This is a race, after all!"

UNDER THE CHECKERED FLAG!

"Worf! Worf!" barked Scuffs as he followed Kin and Junior toward the Waddy Peytona pit area.

"I'm glad to see you, too," Kin said, ruffling the little dog's ears "We've been worried about Laptop, but here he comes."

He pointed to the sky, where a para-glider was slowly circling down.

"Worf!" said Scuffs.

"Here he comes!" yelled Junior.

Junior was talking about Waddy, not Laptop.

Kin readied his sponge-on-a-stick. The Taurus sped into the pit and stopped.

No sooner had the race car stopped than the jack was underneath it. Two cranks of the handle and the car was in the air.

Wielding the torque wrench like a pistol, Junior spun off the lugs. He and his partner moved like lightning, replacing the two right tires. These outside tires got the most wear.

Someday I'll be in the pit with them! vowed Kin. Meanwhile, he carefully swabbed the windshield of the race car with the sponge on the long stick.

Waddy was consulting with Cope.

"It's still heating up," he complained. "I've fallen back to sixth place. By the time we get back in the race, I'll be eighth, with no way to make it up!"

"Darn!" said Cope. "I wish we could figure out what's wrong."

"Worf!"

"What the—??!" said Cope. "Get that darned dog out of here!"

Scuffs had jumped over the pit wall and was barking at the front of the race car.

"No dogs allowed!" said Junior, grabbing at Scuffs.

"Kin, get that mutt out of here!" yelled Waddy.

"Sorry, sir," said Kin. "Scuffs, get back up here behind the wall! Now!"

The little dog paid no attention. Instead, he snapped at the radiator in the front of the Taurus.

"Worf!" said Scuffs, then ran toward Cope.

He had a piece of a transparent plastic bag in his mouth. He offered it to Cope.

"What the—!" said the amazed crew chief.

"Worf worf!" said Scuffs, as the jack let the car down and Waddy roared back into the race.

Cope held up the piece of plastic. "It's warm!" he said.

"He pulled it off the radiator," said Junior. "It must have been stuck there."

"Copacetic! He may have saved the day!"

"Huh?" exclaimed Junior and Kin together.

"This scrap of road trash was blocking the air flow through the radiator. It may be what was making our car overheat!" said Cope.

"It's a little late to find out," said Junior. "Only ten laps to go!"

Laptop almost hated to see the ground. Para-gliding down was so much fun!

And it was simple. He had already gotten the hang of how to make swoops and turns.

His only regret was that he had lost his computer. Not only because it was unique, the only one like it in the world, but also because it was the last legacy of his father.

The race was under the yellow caution flag, and most of the drivers were making pit stops. The fans in the grandstand and the infield were all looking up toward the last act of the "air show."

Laptop went into a tight spiral, vowing to make the last five hundred feet of his para-glide the very best. He swooped low over the grandstand to give the racing fans a thrill.

But something was wrong.

No faces were turned up.

The fans weren't watching the air show anymore.

Then Laptop saw why.

The NASCAR official's green flag was waving wildly—the race was back on, full bore.

Laptop searched for Waddy's car.

There it was—the blue and yellow Ford, moving up through the pack like it was on fire!

Waddy Peytona was in the groove!

The Ford was running perfectly.

"That was it!" said Waddy over the radio. "Whatever you boys did sure fixed the car."

"Copacetic, Waddy!" said Cope, "But it wasn't us boys who did it. We had help."

He winked at the little dog that sat with Kin on top of the pit wall.

"Worf!" said Scuffs.

"What do you mean, you had help?" Waddy asked, his voice crackling over the radio.

"I'll explain later," said Cope. "Don't worry about it now. Just drive. Put the pedal to the metal. Put the hammer down! Let the horses out of the corral!"

Turn three, then turn four.

Then the long straightaway.

The Taurus was running fast and smooth. The tach was reading 6500. The temperature was holding steady. The mighty Ford V-8 was howling.

Waddy Peytona was in the groove.

He slipped past a slow-moving Pontiac on the straightaway, and he was in eighth place. He drafted behind a line of three lapped Pontiacs, then went low at the last instant and left them in the dust, before braking for the sharp angle of turn number one.

Four tires screamed in protest as the Taurus drifted through the curve. Screamed but stuck.

Waddy was in the groove. Unstoppable.

While Jeff Gordon and Terry Labonte duelled for first place, Waddy passed a car the color of pencil lead—the Gray Brothers' Pontiac—and he was in seventh place.

One more pass would put him in sixth. But there were only two more laps to go.

One of the front cars wobbled a little.

Waddy ducked under him, and blasted around.

Sixth place! And only one more lap to go. All he had to do was pass one more car and he was in the money.

But the car was driven by his friend, and rival, Steve Gregson.

Waddy pulled in behind Gregson and drafted on the straightaway—using the Pontiac's airstream to pull him along.

The red and black Pontiac was strong on the short straightaways, but Waddy knew he could pull more rpm's on the home stretch—if he could get around him.

He noticed that Gregson was braking a little early on the steeper turns.

Maybe his brakes are fading, thought Waddy. *That may give me my chance!*

Heading into turn four, Waddy stayed off the brake until the last possible moment—and then stayed off a split second longer.

He dove low, his right front barely scraping Gregson's left rear as the two cars slid into the turn at just under 150 miles per hour.

They came up onto the straightaway side by side.

The Ford was running like a mad beast—turning almost 7000. Waddy knew that this translated into well over 160 miles per hour. At this speed the track looked like a live thing under the wheels of the cars, the black marks on the concrete weaving in and out of one another like long snakes.

Far ahead, Labonte's Chevy was getting the checkered flag.

Waddy had learned long ago to focus his eyes in

the far distance. Anything happening up close was already too late to worry about.

He pulled ahead one foot. Then the Taurus and the Pontiac were running side by side.

Under the checkered flag!

I COULD KILL YOU!

WHOMP!

Laptop tried to stay on his feet, but he fell head over heels in the grass.

He sat up, dazed.

Still alive!

He staggered to his feet. He heard cheering.

He took a bow—then realized that no one was applauding him. The race was over, and the fans were applauding the winners.

He started to fold up his parachute and stuff it into the bag. Then he felt a familiar hand on his shoulder.

"I thought I told you to stay out of trouble!"

It was Hotshoe.

"It wasn't my fault!" protested Laptop.

Laura came running over. "It was so your fault!" she

said. "You told me you would stay by the fence and watch the race. I could kill you."

Laptop looked up at his grandfather and his sister and grinned. "You wouldn't be the first to try today."

Laura and Hotshoe helped Laptop fold the parachute. Then they walked with him toward Infield Annie's.

"I guess I could forgive you," Laura said. "Where's your computer?"

"That's the bad part," said Laptop. "I lost it."

"Lost it?!?" said Hotshoe. "How?"

"It fell. I had to drop it to get the parachute opened." Laptop wiped a tear from his eye. "Now it's gone."

"Is it?" Laura said with a mysterious smile.

They found Annie folding up her mobile kitchen. "I've got something of yours," she said to Laptop.

"You do?"

She handed him a familiar object.

His Apricot 07! He opened it up and turned it on.

It still worked.

He looked from Hotshoe to Laura to Annie. They were all laughing happily. "Where'd you get this?" he asked.

"Let's just say it fell my way," said Infield Annie.

MEET YOUR SPONSOR!

A few minutes later the entire Travis family was gathered at the Victory Lane, watching Terry Labonte collect the trophy for the Pine Gap 300. The driver's weary face was wreathed in smiles.

"Congratulations," said Kin. "Someday I hope to be standing where you're standing."

"I bet you will, too," said Labonte, his eyes twinkling. "Just remember, when you're standing in the Winner's Circle, you're standing on a lot of other folks' shoulders. Racing is a team sport."

"I'll remember that," said Kin, as his little brother joined him.

"Waddy didn't win!" Laptop said, disappointed.

He was surprised to see that neither his brother nor Junior seemed downcast.

"He finished in the top five," said Junior. "That's all that counts. Now we'll have a sponsor."

"And here he is!" said Waddy, who was still covered with grease and oil from the grueling race.

He and Cope shook hands with a man in a white suit and lizard cowboy boots. They were about to introduce him, when they heard a WHUMP! WHUMP! WHUMP!

They all looked up. A helicopter was landing in the infield, right next to the Winner's Circle.

State Trooper Thom was flying the helicopter. The cockpit door opened and Wild Bill jumped out. He ran over to Laptop.

"I need your help," he said. "Did you see where the blimp went with my car?"

"I sure did," said Laptop. "It looked like it crashed into a cliff."

Wild Bill winced in pain. "Can you show us?"

"I—guess." Laptop looked at his grandfather.

"Go on," said Grandpa Hotshoe. "They need your help. But don't be jumping out of any more airplanes—or cars."

Laptop followed Wild Bill to the helicopter and climbed in. "Back in a minute!" he yelled to his grandfather, brother, and sister as the helicopter rose straight into the air.

"Hooray!" shouted the crowd.

They thought it was still another part of the air show!

"Thanks for your help, Kin," said Waddy. "I hope you will be a regular in my pit crew."

"Do you mean *in* the pit?" asked Kin. He wasn't sure he wanted to do the squeegee thing again.

"In the pit for sure," said Waddy. "Whitewall is retiring, and I need another tire man. I am hoping it will be you."

Kin looked at his grandfather. "What do you think?"

"It's a no-brainer," said Hotshoe. "It's the chance of a lifetime. Grab it." He grinned. "Though I think you boys will have a hard time beating Steve Gregson's Pontiac with the new Merlin MixMaster camshaft."

"Isn't that a problem, having two members of the same family on different teams?" asked Laura.

"We're all the same racing family," said Annie. "We compete on the track, but we help each other out in between races. Right, gentlemen?"

"Right as rain," said Gregson and Waddy and Jeff Gordon and Hotshoe all together.

"And now I want you all to meet my new sponsor," said Waddy. He held up the hand of the man in the white suit, as if he were a prizefighter in the ring. "This is Hollis Wabash the Third, the owner and CEO of Wabash Guitars."

Laura was surprised to see the man who had stood in line several times to hear her sing at Infield Annie's.

He smiled at her.

"I'm proud to be sponsoring the great Waddy Peytona Racing Team," said Hollis Wabash III. "We hope to win some races and win some publicity for our fine guitars at the same time. And since you all are one big happy family, perhaps you would be so kind as to introduce me to the young lady who gave us all so much musical enjoyment this afternoon."

"This is Laura Travis," said Annie.

"My granddaughter," said Hotshoe.

"My little sister," said Kin proudly.

"Just sister!" Laura whispered fiercely. "I'm nobody's *little* anything."

"I couldn't help noticing you were playing a beau-tiful Wabash guitar," said Hollis Wabash III. "So I would like to sponsor you, too."

"M-me?"

"And I would like start by asking you to perform at our Smoky Mountain show in Sudden Falls, North Carolina, on Tuesday night," said Hollis III. "It's to honor the families of NASCAR racing."

"Well, sure," said Laura. "I mean, I guess. If—"

"No problem," said Hotshoe. "We'll be traveling through Sudden Falls, and we were planning to attend the show anyway."

"We were?" asked Laura and Kin together.

"Absolutely," said Hotshoe. "I wouldn't miss it for the world."

"Me neither," said Annie.

"I'd be honored to accept, then," said Laura.

She felt a glow steal through her entire body.

Her first professional appearance, on a real stage! And it was only a few days away!

MOVIN' ON

WHUMP!

WHUMP!

WHUMP!

WHUMP!

The helicopter shot upward through the thick summer air.

It was cooler at three thousand feet than it had been down in the bowl of the race track.

Laptop sat between State Trooper Thom and Sheriff "Wild Bill" Wilde.

Ahead was the looming bulk of Rockcastle Mountain. The stone cliffs on the top were wreathed in scraps of cloud.

"Go through that notch," said Laptop. "I saw the blimp go behind that peak, and then hit a cliff."

WHUMP!

WHUMP!

WHUMP!

The helicopter sped through the notch. Trees on either side seemed to be reaching out with their branches to try to swat the swift little machine.

"There!" said Laptop.

He pointed to a narrow ledge halfway up a sheer rocky cliff.

"That ledge is about where the blimp hit," said Laptop.

"I don't see any wreckage," said Trooper Thom.

"My poor car!" said Wild Bill. "It must have fallen into the woods, far below."

The helicopter cruised back and forth over the treetops, but if the car and the blimp had fallen into the forest, they were hidden by the branches.

"Maybe they made it over the top," said Trooper Thom.

"No way," said Laptop. "I saw the blimp heading right for the cliff!"

"Then where's the wreckage?" Wild Bill asked.

"Beats me," said Laptop.

Grown-ups! He knew what he saw. If they didn't want to believe him, that was their problem!

* * * * *

Twenty minutes later, the helicopter was coming in for a landing in the infield of the Pine Gap Raceway.

Wild Bill clapped Laptop on the shoulder.

"Nobody's blaming you, son. You did the best you could. At least you are safe. I don't care that much about the Golden Hawk, honest. It was just . . . just a car."

A tear fell onto his badge, but the rotund lawman kept up a brave front.

The helicopter touched down and Laptop jumped out.

The infield was almost empty.

"Where'd everybody go?" cried Laptop. Infield Annie's tent was gone. So was Waddy Peytona's car hauler.

Laptop waved good-bye to Trooper Thom and Wild Bill as they flew off to continue the hunt for the wreckage of the Golden Hawk.

He found Laura helping their grandfather load his classic 1955 Chevy onto a trailer, to be towed behind his RV.

"After what happened to Wild Bill's Studebaker, I'm not letting this little baby out of my sight," said Hotshoe.

"Good idea," said Kin, who had just walked up. He was covered with grease.

"What happened to you, Kin?" Laura asked, alarmed.

"I'm a pit crew member now," said Kin. "There's a lot of work to do, loading up and moving out. I just helped Junior and Waddy and Cope load the Wabash Guitars Taurus. Now I'll travel with y'all."

"*Y'all?*" said Laptop. "Are you learning to talk Southern or something?"

"Don't worry your little head about it," said Kin. "Now that I'm in a pit crew, I don't think I'll be returning to Boston, that's for sure."

"Boston!" said Laura. "Grandpa Hotshoe, we forgot to return Aunt Adrian's call."

"She'll call back if it's important," said Hotshoe. "Let's load up and get out of here."

"But it *was* important!" said Laura. "She said call her ASAP."

"Don't be such a worrywart," said Kin.

"We have to make it all the way over that mountain to North Carolina," said Hotshoe. He pointed toward Rockcastle Mountain in the distance. "We'd better get moving."

- - - - - - - - - - - - - - - - -

"Let's go, then," said Kin.

The three Travis kids piled into the roomy RV. Hotshoe started the big GM V-8 with a roar.

They were just pulling out when the phone rang.

"Let the machine get it," said Hotshoe. "I can't think of a single soul I want to talk to tonight."

"Worf!" said Scuffs, who always tried to get in the last word.

And they sped off into the mountains, south and east, away from the setting sun.

More later . . .

About the Author

T. B. Calhoun is the pseudonym of an experienced mechanic who has written on automotive topics as well as penned award-winning science fiction and fantasy novels. Like Darrell Waltrip, Jeremy Mayfield, and other NASCAR stars, Calhoun is a native of Owensboro, Kentucky. He currently resides in New York City.

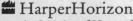

BE A NASCAR WINNER...
With this exciting NASCAR Sweepstakes!

One lucky Grand Prize Winner, along with their parent
or legal guardian, will receive a FREE trip to the official
NASCAR SpeedPark™ in Myrtle Beach, SC
Fifty Second Prize Winners will receive a NASCAR SpeedPark T-shirt.

TO ENTER:

Send in contest entry form located at the back
of NASCAR Rolling Thunder, NASCAR Race Ready,
and NASCAR In The Groove **OR** send a 3 x 5 card
complete with your name, address, telephone
number and birthday to the address below:

Official Rules—

No Purchase Necessary to enter or win a prize. This sweepstakes is open to U.S. residents, 18 years and under, except employees and their families of HarperHorizon/HarperCollins, NASCAR, and their agencies, affiliates, and subsidiaries. This sweepstakes begins on September 9, 1998 and all entries must be received on or before January 1, 1999. HarperHorizon is not responsible for late, lost, incomplete, or misdirected mail. Winners will be selected in a random drawing on or about January 20, 1999 and notified by mail shortly thereafter. Odds of winning depend on number of entries received. All entries become property of HarperHorizon and will not be returned or acknowledged. Entry constitutes permission to use the winner's name, hometown, and likeness for promotional purposes on behalf of HarperHorizon. To claim prize, winners must sign an Affidavit of Eligibility, Assignment and release within 10 days of notification. One Grand Prize of a free trip to the NASCAR SpeedPark in Myrtle Beach, SC will be awarded (approximate retail value $2,000.00) in addition to fifty runner-up prizes of NASCAR SpeedPark T-shirts (approximate retail value $10.00) Total value of all prizes is $2,500. HarperHorizon will provide the sweepstakes winner and one parent or legal guardian with round-trip coach air transportation from major airport nearest winner to Myrtle Beach, SC, 2-day passes into the NASCAR SpeedPark and standard hotel accommodations for a two night stay. Trip must be taken within one year from the date prize is awarded. All additional expenses are the responsibility of the prize winner. One entry per envelope. No facsimiles accepted.

Airline, hotel and other travel arrangements will be made by HarperHorizon in its discretion. HarperHorizon reserves the right to substitute a cash payment of $2,000 for the Grand Prize. Travel and use of hotel and NASCAR SpeedPark are at risk of winner and neither HarperHorizon nor NASCAR SpeedPark assumes any liability.

Sweepstakes void where prohibited. Applicable taxes are the sole responsibility of the winners. Prizes are not transferable and there will be no substitutions of the prizes except at the discretion of HarperHorizon. For the name of the Grand Prize winner send a self-addressed envelope to HarperCollins at the address listed above.

ENTER THE NASCAR SWEEPSTAKES

Mail this entry form along with
the following information to:

**HarperCollins Publishers
10 East 53rd Street
New York, NY 10022
Attn: Department AW**

Name:

Address:

City: State: Zip:

Phone #:   Birthday: /   /